THE
COMPLEX

ALSO BY IAN RANDALL WILSON

Hunger and Other Stories
Absolute Knowledge: Stories
Great Things Are Coming (a novella)
Out of the Arcadian Ghetto (fiction chapbook)
Theme of the Parabola (poetry chapbook)
The Wilson Poems (poetry chapbook)

Praise for *Hunger and Other Stories*

"Wilson pulls at our emotions and hidden desires with a wide variety of characters."
—Annie Sargent, *The St. Augustine Record*

"The writer has a way with words…Each picture is dark with nothingness. The language and sexual scenes makes this adult reading."
—Reba Neighbors Collins, *The Sunday Oklahoman*

"The series of stories has some shining moments of forceful deeply felt description."
—Javier Bernal, *Semana Newspaper*

"These stories are unsettling because of their stark honesty. The frailty of human relationships and the vulnerability of grown-ups spanning a lifetime are a compelling subject."
—Uneza Akhter, *DAWN*

"This amazing use of language, and clarity of description, compels the reader on."
—Patricia Gulian, *Book/Mark*

"The poignant, well-written tales are loaded with depth rarely seen in short stories, turning the reader introspective pondering each story long after finishing them."
—Harriet Klausner, *The Midwest Book Review*

THE
COMPLEX

a novella

Ian Randall Wilson

Hollyridge Press
Venice, California

Hollyridge Press
Venice, California

Cover and Book Design by Rio Smyth
Cover Photo: White Office Building
©Thor Jorgen Udvang | Dreamstime.com
Author Photo by Rebecca Dru

ISBN 10: 0-9843100-8-8
ISBN 13: 978-0-9843100-8-1

23 22 21 20 19 18 17   10 9 8 7 6 5 4 3 2 1

for Denise

*I do not doubt that temporary affairs
keep on and on, millions of years*
—Walt Whitman, *Leaves of Grass*

Acknowledgment

Winner of the 2014 Colony Collapse Novella Prize.

The Complex

THE BLUE CURTAIN HAD MOVED, and K, Jr. was cut off from his usual parking space. With the speed limit posted at 5 MPH, he never left first gear, trolling up and down the aisles, the engine over-revving, driving past rows of Mercedes, BMW's and Saabs. No spaces. His radio played intermittent static and he turned it off. Just then, the first aftershock of the day, the floor swaying, a grim rumble setting off every car alarm in a blare of whoops and shrieks and sirens and buzzers. This was the end of the world, the dagger line three days after what the news in Los Angeles called "the great quake," no counting the tremors, no accounting for the loss of space; the blue curtain stopped him again.

The blue curtain was a large sheet of industrial-grade plastic, weighted at the bottom that hung from ceiling to floor. Full of motion. The officials in Central Distribution offered no explanation for its continuing presence. More than 2 mils thick. It had simply appeared one morning months ago to section off a portion of the underground parking structure, shadow on one side, mystery on the other. It billowed in the middle from breezes that whipped through the structure, their origin unknown, their presence inexplicable as well. Hammering and banging and shouting came from behind the blue curtain but K, Jr. never saw any workmen. Once he had tried to peer behind and was stopped by a guard who said, "This doesn't concern you."

And it moved.

The blue curtain might stay in one place for several days hanging and billowing, its bottom weighted down with the noise of unseen workmen coming from the other side, only to occupy a new spot the next morning. Sometimes it changed places after lunch. Always clean and unwrinkled and brusquely blue. The area previously blocked off appeared unchanged after the departure of the blue curtain. One of the rumors said they were painting the floor, but K, Jr. did not have to look closely to find the gray covering flaking off in scales, black tire tracks crisscrossing the aisles to mark the log lines. Other rumors concerned the installation of surveillance cameras, new lighting, asbestos removal, advanced sprinklers, earthquake shock absorbers, chromium wall coverings, vertical blinds, feather crowns, plaster bats, bomb sniffing canine compounds, soap manufacturing, clay. K, Jr. saw no changes, but whatever its original purpose, he assumed the curtain was now part of the ongoing earthquake repairs. Still, the parking structure grew smaller incrementally as the blue curtain moved less and less, claimed more and more space.

Though he had arrived fifteen minutes early, all the other spaces were filled, forcing him to descend to the next parking level. He rounded the corner to drive down the ramp, the reflection of the blue curtain billowing out caught in his mirror.

The third level was much darker than the ones above. Maintenance hadn't replaced the bulbs, too busy elsewhere in The Complex working on the broken doors, the cracked windows, the elevators that stuck, evaluating structural integrity, fencing off the vertical load carrying systems; life. No cars were parked down here, yet all of the spaces had small metal signs suspended overhead marked *Reserved for P. Levitt, Reserved for R. Alexander, Reserved for D.L. Stevens, Reserved for A. Chacon, Reserved for E.E.M. Wood*. Even the handicap spot had a placard saying *Reserved for Bursky.* A memo had been circulated expressly forbidding parking in reserved spaces by anyone other than the re-servee. Tow-trucks would be called, fines levied, parking privileges revoked. Don't do it! K, Jr. drove and drove and drove, up and down the aisles, maintaining the posted 5 MPH speed, searching for an unreserved space. Each turn brought him farther away from the light.

He parked, finally, in the farthest most north-ern corner of the structure, next to a pile of refuse that appeared ready to topple at any moment. He had his headlights on now, easing into the space still unsure of its legitimacy. The lack of a reserva-tion sign overhead, however, gave him hope. When he turned off the lights and the engine, he was consumed by the darkness of the corner, a gloom so pervasive that the weak light of the ele-vator bank, only a hundred yards away, seemed miles and miles removed.

K, Jr. locked his car and went to the eleva-tors which occupied a concrete and cinderblock lobby in the middle of the structure. He heard the booming sound of the mysterious work going on behind the blue curtain. A rush of the phantom winds found their way three floors below ground level. K, Jr.'s feet scraped the pavement. He was completely alone.

He pushed the up button and nothing happened. It was not unusual for the lights to remain unlit; these bulbs too, might be burned out—or the elevators might not be working. He couldn't be sure.

K, Jr. waited five minutes and pushed the button again. He allowed another two before he became convinced that the elevators were out of service. Elevator service had been a problem in The Complex even before the earthquake. Another memo said it was one of the infrastructure problems that was being attended to, along with overhead lighting and inferior photocopying equipment. Please be patient!

So many problems on a Monday, so much to do upstairs, the Memo in its final stages of preparation and McPursky sure to be upset at K, Jr.'s lateness.

He went back across the parking structure floor to a staircase that promised ground level access only. Lateness was unusual for K, Jr. He pressed hard on the safety bar across the door and forced it open. Another memo had chided the staff for their tardiness. Be on time! The emergency stairwell was brightly lit. K, Jr. tried to follow the dictums, but not this morning. His footsteps resounded on the metal staircase as he walked resolutely up. There was evidence of non-structural damage from the accumulation of aftershocks: the stairway had pulled away from the wall in places, dust littered the floor, certain precast concrete elements had cracked, the ceiling gaped, water pipes had split leaving a trail down the walls; but the lights worked extremely well. The stairs led upward in a series of ninety degree turns, each turn punctuated by a metal landing with an upraised tread pattern for safe footing.

K, Jr. carried a briefcase in his left hand, held the railing with his right. His heart rate and breathing increased as he clanked up the stairs. He paused after two flights to catch his breath. At the top of the third he tried the door but it was locked. No amount of pushing could open it.

Stuck in a crack in the concrete was what looked like a baseball card. He pulled it out and discovered it was a Saint card. There was a drawing of St. Emicus, patron saint of the unemployed. Below the rendering were all the vital statistics: date of birth and death, country of origin, holy work that had earned him saint-hood, the method of martyrdom—St. Emicus had been swallowed by the earth. Everywhere he looked the earthquake produced a cinematic fiction in black and white and shadow. He stuck the card back into the crack. How did one enter silence, cross a dark street, fix on the solid core? Thinking now would not restore the world.

He was twenty minutes late and wondering why they had been called back to work while the city counted backwards, the earthquake initiating a reverse in progress: streets collapsed, water mains ruptured, gas lines exploded into orange flames bearing pale blue centers, buildings bent in and had to be condemned. They were razed overnight, the twisted steel carted off, dust and piles of bricks remaining.

What universe can withstand the pressure of its souls?

He retraced his steps downward, trying the door to the next level. He pushed on it, rattled the handle, pushed again bringing down a shower of dust, but it refused to open. The banging continued, somewhere, up above, the blue curtain was moving.

At the elevator bank the call button lit on the first push. Someone had posted a memo. Expect delays! Fifteen seconds later the doors slid open, the elevator compartment empty. K, Jr. pushed the button for the fifth floor, the doors slid closed, the elevator began to move upward.

Then the lights on the panel flashed, the elevator lurched, stopped somewhere between the second and third floors of the building, and descended, opening its doors to the lowest parking level. It waited, doors open, control panel inoperative. K, Jr. stepped off.

Once more he pushed the call button, firmly, with a rigid index finger. The doors to the elevator slid closed. A few moments later they opened and this time the compartment was completely filled with people.

"Are you going up?" K, Jr. said.

"Where else would we be going you idiot. Sideways?"

"Indeed," said K, Jr. "Good morning, Christian."

"Screw you."

"Nice weekend?"

Christian was apparently not coping well with the stress from the earthquake and the subsequent aftershocks which occurred every day. K, Jr. started to say something, stopped, didn't think it proper in front of all these people, thought he had to, didn't. By then, the elevator was already rising smoothly. A young woman that K, Jr. recognized from secretarial services burst into tears.

She ran off the elevator as soon as the doors opened and Christian said, "That was one of your longer relationships."

"Screw you," said K, Jr.

"What a way you have with women. I think I can learn from you. Exactly what did you say to her?"

They got off together at the fifth floor entering a lobby full of portable heater-fans blowing tremendous gusts of fetid air over the wet carpets. A memo had explained that a number of outside agencies had been contracted to repair and refurbish the facility though business had been resumed following a structural examination of The Complex. Pardon our dust! Giant yellow tubes snaked from blue equipment into offices. Cold air rushed in through gaping spaces in windows that had burst from the pressure.

"She doesn't seem to be coping too well with the earthquake either." K, Jr. had to yell over the sound of the fans and the drying equipment.

"What do you mean either?" Christian shouted.

K, Jr., trailed by Christian, navigated around workmen in blue hard-hats who marched by in each direction wearing blue shirts and blue suspenders. His shoes had just been polished. The men wore paint-covered tool belts slung low on the hips dragging down their jeans. His pants, freshly pressed, began getting dirty. In the fatter men, the cleft of hairy backsides peeked through. Attractive. Tape measures and hammers and all kinds of other tools were stuck in the leather holders. Their workboots were marked with plaster dust, seamed by hard labor.

"What do you mean?" Christian said. "Either? What are you saying?"

Three lefts and a right down a poorly-lit corridor brought them to K, Jr.'s office, past more plastic yellow tubes now joined by a clear one that fluttered from the air blowing through them. They had to step over tubes and wires and extension cords. They had to walk around dollies full of plasterboard and lath, past buckets full of cloudy water. They left footprints on the carpet.

"My drive was terrible," K, Jr. said. "It's terrible out there."

"What do you mean either?"

They stood in front of K, Jr.'s office which had, miraculously suffered little damage. Most of his books had fallen and one of the file drawers had toppled but K, Jr. had fixed that up in a couple of hours. He had been one of the first to resume working.

With his right hand, Christian tapped against the glass of K, Jr.'s door. Incessant tapping. Workmen were clearing out the office next door.

"What happened to McFarland?" K, Jr. said.

"What do you mean either?"

"Did you get through it all right? I had some pretty big cracks in the walls and in the corners. A couple of the bookcases broke. No structural damage otherwise. They've green tagged the building and we're waiting for the landlord to make repairs."

"I'm doing fine. My wife and I. We're doing fine. We came though it fine. The house is fine. Our relationship is fine. I'd say we're fine. Very fine." The tapping continued.

"Why was McFarland fired?"

"McFarland is out. McManus, McMahon, McCormick, and McRickland."

"When did this happen?"

"McP may be in trouble also. Let's go get donuts."

K, Jr. said no and entered his office. He was too late already and a memo had been circulated outlining the policy on coffee breaks which restricted them to later in the morning, and in the afternoon. Two breaks only, ten minutes please!

Christian said, "I've heard some other rumors which I think we should discuss. We need to strategize. Pool our resources."

They were still yelling over the sound of the drying equipment.

"Later," K, Jr. said, and closed his door reducing the noise outside to a friendly level, insistent but manageable. He turned on the overhead lights, the banker's light on the desk, the lamp in the corner, his computer, his monitor, his printer, his typewriter, his adding machine, his transcriber, took the phones off forward, changed the dates on his receipt stamps, readjusted the materials on his desk which were disturbed each night by the clean-up crew, turned the monitor a half-inch to the right, straightened the keyboard, replaced the software template above the keys, adjusted the wrist-rest to the proper typing angle.

The frame holding a picture of his girlfriend, Ramona, had fallen over. She was short with brown hair and brown eyes and, in the picture, her face was placed flat against a wall. She told him it was an "artistic" shot, that he had a fine eye for composition. Perhaps he should be doing something else besides his work with numbers. "What might that be?" he said.

K, Jr. picked up the frame and placed it at the farthest left corner of the desk so she was always visible to him. He called her but only got her voice mail. "It's a mess here," he said to the recording. "I was thinking of you."

How could one go on living in the city? Two years ago, the city burned, or so it seemed behind the glass of a twenty-seven inch Zenith. Nine channels of mayhem, no commercials. It would be impossible to sell beer against the panicked overhead shots from Chopper 2, the pilot's voice broken by the engine noise, shouting that the building is burning, the crowd is looting, the police are not around—as if K, Jr. could not see for himself this elegant madness through the smoke, children carrying toasters leaping through a gap in the security fence, adult faces grim with the weight of their boxes, dragging new televisions home. The looters were all black or brown, and when they made it to the street, they laughed. A couple of men danced. One shook his fist at the helicopter. K, Jr. had food, and didn't need to go out. But in the watching, a new recognition of home emerged. The walls were thin and there was little insulation. Outside and inside merged easily in the light of a match, in the openings of broken glass, in the fervor of hooded figures dancing. Fire became fire became fire, who saw the edges anymore?

One year later, arsonists used flares to set fire to dry brush near a grade school. It burned well. The winds swept off the desert, pace increased by the constriction of narrow canyons and the rising heat. The wildfires north of Los Angeles moved twelve miles in four hours linking up with the coast, turning east toward the densely residential places. City of Angels, city of riots, city of smoke. As if to emphasize the separateness of lives, the social connections occurring on the street were severed with the fire's threat. People kept their heads down, fought over jugs of water in the stores. They raided the supermarket shelves for food, ran the reds driving home. It was everyone for themselves, charting the burning down the coast. Soon, we will all be threatened. A fireman described it as something live, something breathing, evil and purely destructive—without a soul. K, Jr. was up all night, watching smoke-streaked faces on nine channels of fire. Without a soul. This fire has no soul, the anchors announced. It is the great leveler. The whole city burned, or so it seemed to watch the thing in restless fascination, houses livid against a backdrop of intense yellow, boundless immolation, the yellow drew him, the spit and curl of flame; he felt its heat, desire in the glowing.

Now more fires. The trembling earth. Buildings swaying, breaks in the street. Nights without sleeping. Friends called, suggesting he leave before the earth opened, finally, to swallow them whole, before the city dropped into the ocean, before the really big one came. And go where? Do what?

McPursky stopped him in the hallway. "What about the numbers? Have you found the sums? Have you moved everything? Do the columns line up? We can't have any bare spots. I need results."

"There was a delay in audit 2. I've called them and they promise."

"No excuses. We're a team here. I need results. How is your family?"

"I'm sorry?"

"These things matter. I hope you're spending time with the family."

"I'll have more numbers for you later today, Mr. McPursky."

"That's the stuff I like to hear. Good stuff. Smart stuff. Street stuff. Go, team, go."

Christian was in the kitchen. "There's no coffee and McPursky is out."

"How can that be?"

Christian shrugged. "Word is that McTate is out as well and the board is bringing in a whole new group to run the place. There will be blood. Blood in the hallways. Blood on the walls. I predict a wholesale slaughter. Your little memo..."

"It's not my memo. It's a departmental memo. It's McPursky's memo. He thought it up, designed it, decided it mattered. I'm only responsible for columns 5 and 6."

"Yes, yes. I'm worried about you, son. You should know that you're not alone. We're all feeling this stress, whether we admit it or not. But you have to be aware of possible aftereffects: anger, irritability, disbelief, shock, rage, nightmares, sleeplessness, hyperactivity, headaches, dizziness, and nausea."

"I'm not pregnant. I'm waiting for more files."

"I'm sure you are."

A memo had been circulated about dealing with the aftereffects from the earthquake. Many resources were listed including banks offering interest-free loans and doctors helping with special counseling. We're in this together!

Christian leaned in close and put his hand on K, Jr.'s shoulder. "When McTate goes, the whole group goes with him. Plan on changing. Study up. Stay current. Keep your resume on file. We're out of coffee. I'm going downstairs."

The second aftershock came at 10:30, shaking the building enough to bring down the florescent light fixture in front of the door. K, Jr. was at his desk, diligently moving the numbers from column five into column six. It was painstaking work. He had piles of papers in front of him delivered twice a day from the file room, files in crisp, clean, cream-colored binders delivered twice a day. He had never completely understood what the company did; no one completely understood what the company did. Something about arts funding and ethnographic studies. They charted populations distribution by streets, income by trees, placed the axis of cable distribution nodes on the vertical against a horizontal shift of families who preferred fish on Fridays to those who ate it twice a month. Numbers and tables and lists and files and K, Jr. was responsible for columns five and six. A memo had circulated outlining this year's activities, but he didn't have enough time to read the reports and was never able to draw conclusions or infer trends from the numbers. This is us! They were all different. They formed no cohesive pattern. They were symbols that he moved, carefully, deliberately, faithfully. Beyond that, they didn't signify.

The aftershock came at 10:30 and K, Jr. mistyped a seven. The light fell from the ceiling and hung, suspended by wires, its activator buzzing, edges tilting left and right like a kite as the rumbling died off. The door burst open, slamming into the wall, the handle gouging out another piece of plaster from the wall where it had previously impacted. A memo had circulated outlining minor repair procedures. Fill out a report! Three men from Maintenance entered, one carrying a ladder, one carrying a bucket, another with a package of long thin glass bulbs wrapped in cardboard.

"Ponga la escalera ahi."

"Hay algun daño?"

K, Jr. jumped. "What?" he said, standing now. He had no Spanish, the language eluded him as did the numbers. Nothing signified.

"Note sentes en tu escritorio. Listos a que se del escritorio."

"¿Esta es la oficina numero 5197?"

"Estamos equivocados de lugar."

"Estamos en el lugar correcto."

"Quinté preguntó?"

"Perdoné la molestia."

"The wall," K, Jr. said. "Look at the wall."

Then he pointed at the light but they ignored him. They set up the ladder, took turns examining the damage. They wore gray jumpsuit-uniforms with white patches above the heart, a place for their names. The man who carried the ladder was the first to climb, one step at a time, checking his footing carefully, testing his weight, unwilling to move upward before he confirmed that the ladder would hold. When he climbed off, the man who carried the bucket began upward. Unbalanced and wobbling with each step, he held his hands out to the side as if trying to maintain his equilibrium on a tightrope. He spent very little time inspecting the light, much more trying to stay on the ladder and not fall off. The man who had carried the light bulbs was the last up. He boldly placed his foot on each step, moving upward with grace and straight posture, his head erect.

"Hay algun daño?"

"Quinté preguntó?"

"Hokay, mister," the man who carried the ladder said. And then they caucused close together like a small football huddle, whispering, none of the Spanish was K, Jr. able to make out. The man who had carried the light bulbs was designated to return the light to the fixture. Again he climbed the step ladder, the other men shouting:

"Si."

"Isquierdo. Isquierdo. Isquierdo!"

"Quinté preguntó?"
"Para derecho. Si."
"Si. Para derecho."

The man on the ladder ignored both of the other workers and simply pushed the assembly back into the fixture where it fit easily although the activator continued to buzz.

"What about the noise?" K, Jr. said. "The noise. You can't just leave it like this. What are your names? Don't leave. You have to do something."

The man in charge of the ladder folded the ladder and backed out of the room. The man with the bucket picked up the bucket and backed out the room. The man in charge of the lights stepped out of the room, picked up his package of long glass tubes and walked away.

"Perdoné la molestia."
"Perdoné la molestia."
"Perdoné la molestia."

K, Jr. came around his desk and out into the hall.

"The noise?" he said. "The noise. I can't work with that buzzing going on. Don't you hear it? Please. Can't you just look at it a little more closely. It shouldn't take too long."

K, Jr. looked furtively up and down the hallway. Then he said, "I could pay something, a little extra, for your trouble."

"Hay un reporte y lo investigaramos."

"What? What?"

"Perdoné la molestia," The man carrying the ladder shouted and they rounded a corner, disappearing from view.

K, Jr. stood at the door for ten minutes moving in and out of a reverie. He pressed his thumbs into the cool black metal of the door-frame, pressing and releasing. He stroked the smooth sides with the tips of his fingers. He left circular prints that stayed for a moment recording the whirls of his fingers, then evaporated as if they had never been.

They hadn't understood him. He hadn't understood them. They didn't understand the importance of work. He didn't know how busy they might be. McFarland had complained that Maintenance refused to learn English. McFarland had been let go. McFarland, K, Jr. was led to understand, was responsible for columns 1 and 2, but only the even pages. Someone else, on another floor, in another building, had the odd pages. "Sometimes he gets confused," McFarland said.

"Does my pages. I've complained about that too."
McFarland complained. McFarland was let go.
The activator buzzed. Sometimes the light flickered.
The prints vanished as if they had never been.

K, Jr. was about to go back to his work
when he saw Ramona's picture was again face
down, except now there was a small statue of
the Virgin Mary on top of the metal. She cra-
dled a baby to her breast. She was not weeping.

He tossed the statue in the trash and went
back to copying numbers from column five to
column six, though the buzzing gave him a
headache. He believed in the privilege of man
and had no time for organized religion. He
stopped frequently to rub his eyes and his temples, took off his glasses, pressed at the bridge
of his nose. His morning's output was greatly
reduced as a result. McPursky was sure to notice, the Memo would be held up. K, Jr. would
be responsible. Terrible, how terrible.

In the afternoon, Ramirez was let go. He
stood just inside the door of his office loading
books from the shelves into boxes, emptying
drawers of small rubber-banded stacks of papers, removing a pen and pencil set off the top
of his desk, taking pictures off the walls. A

memo had circulated advising of the proper way to pack and remove boxes from the building. State your name! Ramirez was in violation. He taped the boxes closed, unmarked, and stacked them up next to the door.

"The mailroom boy said he'd come up with a dolly and help me carry this stuff out. I still need a property removal pass, though, can you imagine? I don't know how all of this accumulated. I don't even remember bringing half of it in, and I just finished getting back on the shelves in the proper order. Why didn't they just do this right after the quake, really make it hurt."

K, Jr. tried to find something to say and thought only of worn-out homilies, stock phrases from impotent clerics that neither comforted nor helped.

He said, "Is there anything I can do to help?"

K, Jr. felt a certain affinity for Ramirez—a real affinity, he decided—the other man worked on something totally different. But Ramirez's wife had just had twins and he delighted in showing off pictures to K, Jr. and some of the others nearby. Who could resist?

"I'm sure you'll find something," K, Jr. said.

"I'm sure I will."

"Yes, I'm sure you will."

"I will."

"Will you start looking immediately?"

Ramirez held up his hand. "We'll be all right. I've managed to save a few pfennigs from the lousy pay they give us here. You really should think about getting out. A man of your talents has much more to offer than this."

Ramirez spread his hands around the office which had begun to look barren and sterile as every sign of its inhabitant's life went into the boxes.

"I'm sure there's so much more you could be doing," Ramirez said. "They don't treat us, I mean you, right here. Your efforts have clearly been unappreciated. I'm not entirely sure what you do, K—"

"Who among us is."

"That's funny. Very funny. See, not only great competence but a man with a sense of humor. You have a perspective on life and that is so important. I tell my wife that about you all the time. I tell her that I'm next to man with a sense of humor and a man who has a perspective on life.

She wants to know on which side is the man with the sense of humor on which side is the man with perspective on life. She has a sense of humor too, you see. No matter how many times I tell her that it's all the same man, she asks me on which side, Ramirez, on which side?"

Suddenly Ramirez staggered and sat down in his chair. He held his hand over his face. He dropped the scissors and tape to the floor as if they had suddenly grown too heavy to hold. His complexion darkened, the muscles in his cheeks twitched, his eyes squeezed tightly shut. K, Jr. was about to come to him and again he held up his hand.

"No, no," Ramirez said. "I hate for you to see me this way. Hate it. Absolutely. I'm going to miss this place terribly. I don't want to admit that to myself but the best times I had in my working career were in this place. Great friends. Great times."

"It hasn't been that long," K, Jr. said. "You'll find something."

"Find something. Right. It'll never have the same charm or autonomy."

"It'll be better."

"That's what I mean about you, you're an optimist, too. These are such important qualities in a man. I wish I had them. I don't want to keep you anymore. I'm sure there are other things you need to be working on. Please. You don't mind if I call you from time to time? Just to keep in touch with the old gang? I'd like that."

"Of course."

K, Jr. put in a good hour of work moving numbers. When the work went well there was a rhythm to the transfers. He spotted sequences and was able to shift them to the next column smoothly and without interruption. He input the numbers without looking—and they were always right. Sevens appealed to him most, the sprightly uprightness, their turn to the left. Fours were second best, again it was their thrusting upward that lent them charm.

But when the work went poorly K, Jr. had to consult the originals again and again. Remembering even two numbers became a burden. They slipped from his mind like the water through his fingers in the washroom when he splashed his face to revive himself. He went from the list to the keyboard to the screen back to the list. Then only zeros counted. He could hold them, maintain their shape. In all situations, zeros had integrity.

A delivery arrived from the mailroom, yet another new face behind the cart, this one, a wickedly thin young man with black hair plastered back against his head.

"Did you just join us?" K, Jr. said.

"I've been here three years."

"Really. I'm used to the usual man. What's his name? Philip."

"William."

"William," said K, Jr.

"On the night shift.

"William?"

"Me. I've been on the night shift," the mail boy said. He handed over a group of files and then a bundle of envelopes held together with a rubber band. "Typing mostly. That's why you haven't seen me. I'm having trouble with my hands. The syndrome. You need to watch out for that." He picked up a group of files from the outbox and put them in his cart. He also picked up several inter-offices envelopes. "These are mislabeled," he said. "You've made a mistake. It's good you have a wrist-rest. I never used one. I was sure nothing was going to happen to me."

A memo had been circulated regarding the proper labeling and addressing of inter-office mail. Mark the room number! "I can't take them, the mail boy said," and put the letters back in the tray. "Stupid. I'll get them the next run. I was convinced I was invulnerable."

"Those letters need to go out."

"I used to time myself. Fix the labels. I'll get them the next run. I got up to 130 words a minute."

"Amazing."

The mail boy looked at him sharply. "With only three mistakes."

"Impressive. How about now? How fast can you type?"

"I'm not so young you see. Not anymore."

K, Jr. began looking at the files just delivered while the younger man talked. K, Jr. broke in suddenly. "These files are the same ones I had picked up this morning. Why are you bringing them back?"

"Impossible. They were in your box marked for delivery."

"There's been a mistake."

"We don't make mistakes. I should know. I've been here three years. No mistakes in all of that time. The ones who make mistakes are let go and as I am still here you can see that I don't make mistakes."

"We have to call someone."

"You can, if you want to. Personally, I think that would be a mistake. Questioning what Central Distribution gives you to work on can get you labeled."

"I've been here much longer than you and I think I know what I'm supposed to be working on, better than you might."

"I'm only trying to help. You clerks are all alike. You think you're doing important work." The mailroom boy held up his hands. "I thought I was doing important work too. See how swollen they are. I sacrificed these for the company. My youth. Gone. 130 words a minute. Close to a record. Now do you want me to take the files back or leave them? I have a lot of other deliveries to do, important deliveries. And I don't have time to be talking to someone who questions whether or not I'm doing my job."

"Leave them. All right. Leave them."

"Someone should be questioning the kind of job you're doing. You have no sense of humor, do you know that? Even if these are the wrong files you might look at it as a joke. Isn't life a joke? I'm wasting my time."

He walked up the hall, angrily pushing his mail cart before him, banging the wheels into the walls, slapping doors, muttering.

K, Jr. consulted his directory. At what level to make his complaint? The head of the mailroom? The head of operations? The vice president of Central Distribution? The head of the fileroom?

He began thinking of what to say, was led into a reverie about his own first few weeks at the company. He made plenty of mistakes but they always gave him another chance. Then he learned, and was rewarded. There was a form to fill out for misdeliveries. A memo had been circulated changing the distribution process. Effective immediately, everyone who had previously contacted Cathy Banolis at International Services should contact Rick Andoval at Worldwide Services, which is the new name of International and Domestic Services following the dissolution and merger of these two groups. Questions? Call Rick! He was not available. He might be in later. K, Jr. was invited to leave a message and the assistant would see to it that Rick tried to get back to him as soon as possible, though there were forty-two others on the call sheet from the morning alone and Rick was still hard-pressed to return any of his calls from last week what with the power going in and out and the uncertainty of the phone system, or better still, the assistant suggested sending a memo through the inter-office mail, properly labeled of course to insure quick and appropriate delivery, which would set forth the problem, as K, Jr. was experiencing it, in the clearest detail and obtain the quickest response, but that K, Jr. should be aware that the staff was currently experiencing a personnel problem with the effects and after-effects of the recent disaster and that no one could be assured of a timely response in the face of a *force majeur* event such as this one. Did he want to leave word?

An hour later K, Jr. observed boxes being dropped off for Weinstein who was directly across the hall. K, Jr. came around from his desk and went to his door. Weinstein was furiously putting the boxes together, ripping at the cardboard, bending the flaps in the wrong direction. He too, was not properly labeling his boxes.

K, Jr. said, "They may not let those boxes out if they're incorrectly labeled."

"Are you working for Building Services now?" Weinstein said. "Becoming their watch-dog? I bet you had something to do with this."

"Whatever can you mean?" K, Jr. said. "Do with what? I'm just trying to be helpful. I've heard you need a property removal pass as well."

"This. I've been given an hour to pack. Can you imagine the indignity of it all. An hour, after five years of service."

"I thought the information might be help-ful. It's terrible that you've been let go. I'm sorry for you."

"Save your pity. They've given me my ac-crued vacation time and a week for every year of service. There are no jobs out there. I'll be standing on street corners with a sign that says 'Will Work For Food'. The horror of it."

"If I see you, I'll give you some spare change."

"That kind of deliberate black humor is not at all appreciated. I hope no one who matters hears you because it could get you into serious trouble. Serious."

"But you'll find something."

"Don't say that to me. Don't try to mollify me with your ridiculous Pollyanna attitude toward life. No one finds something. Without family connections or knowing someone, nothing just comes. I had a better offer last month. Damned if I shouldn't have taken it. You know it's your optimism that's holding you back. If you'd take a hard-nose approach you might be getting somewhere in this business. You've been here longer than me and what do you have to show for it?"

"I'm happy with my progress. The people I work for appreciate me."

"There you go again. They use you like an animal of burden and when they've wrung every last bit of work out of you, they toss you to the side. Promises were made to me too, promises that were not kept. Have they made the same to you?"

When K, Jr. did not answer right away Weinstein said, "Huh, I thought so. You're as blind as all the rest. Wait. You'll see. You think work on your memo is going well—"

"How do you know about that?"

"You think I don't know. You think I'm the idiot across the hall. I know. I know a lot things. I suggest you start thinking metric. Learn Spanish so you can speak to those idiots in Maintenance. Who do you think really runs this company? You're going to need those talents much quicker than you know."

"Excuse me, but I have a lot of work to do. I hope that you find something. I could offer a letter if that would help."

"Don't insult me. A letter from you? What good would that do? Everyone has your number."

He turned his back and resumed hurling his personal belongings into the boxes. K, Jr. returned to office. But his work went slowly. The numbers were difficult to copy. The light was bad. He had trouble reading. The activator buzzed. McFarland this morning. He decided not to fill out a report. He had filled out three about the hole in the wall and that was not repaired. McFarland complained about things like that. McFarland was let go. Ramirez after lunch and now Weinstein. They were not from his group but K, Jr. had observed over the time he'd been with the company, the years he had worked in The Complex that lay-offs came in waves and every department at every level was affected.

The boy from the fileroom came back. "It turns out you were correct. A mix-up. A new employee put the same files back into your slot instead of the return slot. I had nothing to do with it. Nothing whatsoever. And I would thank you not to mention this incident to anyone. If you know what I mean."

"I've already called Rick."

"Rick? Rick can't help you. I heard he was laid-off this morning. A number of people were laid-off this morning. And more are coming."

"Do you know something?"

"Isn't that just like you, going behind my back, trying to get me in trouble. And I had nothing to do with it. Nothing. I deliver what they give me. That's all."

"You're just repeating rumors."

"I happen to know. You hear things in this job. Important things. The men in the mailroom know. You should believe me, because I know."

"How do I explain this mistake to my superiors? I've been reworking the same files all afternoon."

"That's not my problem. I didn't have anything to do with it. The worker who made the mistake is sorry and will be disciplined appropriately, I'm led to understand. You'll have to make do. Now give me the files so I can return them."

"What about the files I was supposed to be working on. You've set me back a whole day." K, Jr. picked up the phone.

"Don't call anyone. Look what happened to Rick. Don't tell anyone."

"Are you suggesting there's some kind of connection? What a stupid—"

"I have a lot of friends in The Complex. It could go badly for you."

"Are you threatening me?"

"I'm telling you how things are. I've been here three years. I know about these things."

"Get out of my office. What's your superior's name? Never mind. I'll find out myself. Get someone else to bring me my files from now on. I don't intend to deal with you anymore."

The boy from the fileroom started laughing. "You clerks are all alike. Self important. Wait. Your time is coming."

K, Jr. found himself staring off, regarding the door, his lips separated. He had stopped sleeping or he had forgotten how to sleep or had never slept or he still possessed the concept of sleep, one involving sheets and goose down, but it resided in the distant memory of things that used to be along with solid walls, bedrock, and the peace following an end to motion. He might be awake now, remembering the properties of stillness. But when the outlines of consciousness soften, where does a world begin?

The aftershocks landed with regularity each day, the moment of their intrusion more predictable than love. But there was no knowing their forms: once the subtle shift of the building, twice a grinding, then an overt smash that struck at noon like the slap of flat palms, and moved on. At home he had lost count of the cracks, the walls crazed with horizontal lines by the door matching horizontal lines outside. He inferred a connection.

He had friends who could write down their dreams. They believed the psyche spoke to them in darkness. His balance had been upset, the cornice torn, the angles changed. The load-bearing surfaces held, it was the decorative aspects thrown off-center.

The ground had fallen. These same friends called it a settling process. They believed the restoration of power made everything whole. Yet both sides of the city had been severed when the 10 Freeway collapsed over a patch built on marshland. Repairs would take a year. There were no links between east and west. Strange that no one remembered *la cienega* meant "the swamp." This was a festival for the building trades.

The doctors offered free help; K, Jr. realized he had abandoned medication too soon. In the City of Angels clerics called it the fifth sign of the apocalypse, two more to the next coming which they struggled to predict. Reason withered in the lack of dreaming. A notice said beware of irritability. He no longer wished to be married. His interests were in the immediate. He felt a more murderous kind of rage.

News fractured into pictures of general suffering, an editorial describing it as the City of Angles. He could not eat quickly enough now seven years in a dry drunk wasting for sleep. In his office, he lay his head down and pressed his face into the cool wood of his desk. Concentration was an illusion; they should be released from work. The phones rang too loud.

To speak of this as a mere disruption was to equate the destruction of planets with pressing dough. He was out of conclusions. He consid-

ered leaving, evaluated the levy of staying behind. The cracks had transformed him, walls
crumbled. A floor remained beyond which they
go no lower. With the earth in motion, even
this was a dream.

At 6 o'clock, K, Jr. made a differential back-
up of his hard drive, signed off the network,
placed the files he had just completed in the
out box, closed the files he was working on and
put them into an orderly pile on the credenza
behind his desk, locked his drawer, put on his
coat, pushed in his chair, and shut off the light.
He decided to wait, not make a complaint, test
the tenor of things tomorrow when the light
was better, his thoughts clearer.

One of the older secretaries walked by. She
carried two reams of Xerox paper poorly hidden
under her coat. She stared straight ahead obvi-
ously trying to pretend she didn't see him and
he didn't see her. The bundles were too heavy
for her and she listed to the right.

As he made his way down the hall, computers were being turned off, fans stopping,
motors running down, chairs rolling, lights
extinguishing, doors closing. Three offices
away, K, Jr. saw a man he didn't know stuffing

his pockets with pens and paperclips, bottles of liquid paper and small bundles of index cards. His suit coat bulged giving him the appearance of breasts. There were strange lumps in his pants. A memo had been circulated about such theft. Thou shalt not steal! The man looked when K, Jr. walked past but didn't stop loading up.

The elevators were working well and answered the call button quickly. In the parking garage K, Jr. saw a man parked in the handicap spot loading a typewriter into his trunk. The man slammed the trunk shut, looked around then quickly got into his car. He backed up fast, put the car into gear, the tires squealing.

There was a flier tucked under his windshield wiper announcing the end of the world, salvation through Our Lord. The answer. K, Jr. crumpled it into a ball, tossed it into the back of car and joined a line of traffic waiting to get out of the structure. A memo had circulated about driving in the parking garage. Keep to the left! There was a steady, uninterrupted flow of traffic passing before the exit to the building. The ramp was steep and K, Jr. had his left foot on the brake, the right one ready on the gas so the car would not roll back. Someone honked behind him, then pulled out and whipped by. Tires squealed. Horns blared. Someone shouted, Idiot. Get out of the way. Learn how to drive. Go back to New York.

K, Jr. kept to the speed limit. Since the earthquake a week before, people were not driving well. They turned unexpectedly. They stopped for no reason. They were unaware that their cars had no brake lights and did not seem at all grateful when that fact was politely pointed out to them.

K, Jr. prepared to make a left in a large intersection. From the opposite direction a car sailed through, running the red light, nearly broadsiding him. He was startled. He hit the brake, the gas, turned the wheel. The car stalled. Horns blared. A hand was extended outside a window giving K, Jr. the finger. Mercy.

A police car blocked his lane up ahead. K, Jr. signaled and attempted to merge into the right lane. A large red convertible blocked him and refused to let him in.

"Why are you driving like that?" K, Jr. shouted.

"I don't like the way you drive, shithead," the driver said.

K, Jr. let the man pass, rolled up his window and merged behind. He took the next right, anything to get off this street, away from the traffic. It took a long time to get home.

Across the street, tents had been erected. Hundreds gathered in the park in a loose assembly of disorder. Soldiers wearing camouflage fatigues stood in glazed boots on guard. They handed out food, slinging their rifles behind in an effort to reduce the menace. Many of these newly homeless had escaped from a building damaged next door. A bullhorn announced, "We will allow you access to the third floor only, in a series of fifteen minute intervals; please be prompt."

This was occurring all over the city. K, Jr. watched, briefly, on the news, these scenes framed in the context of adventure—until the rain began and the canvas leaked. Only luck divided them from him, a random choice of housing. We are given to the world in the sudden way events are displaced from the known axis to reiterate what history tells us has already occurred. Fire, famine, flood, now the earth's undulation sends so many into the streets. The man with bullhorn in the park said, "The heavy items are lost to you, perhaps you can reclaim some books."

Under convenient canvas stretched by wood poles, in the primitive encampment fortified by portable generators that raised enough current for light, home became a process. The authorities encouraged an expanded definition of the place where one lives. Now the sides were green, and coarse, still softer than stone. K, Jr.'s power had been restored, no hot water. His possessions filled his shelves. The man with the bullhorn said, "We will allow you to pick through the rubble of anything remaining; this is as close as you can get."

That expanding definition eliminated attachments to what was known. How then, does one make a life in a dividing universe where the thing thought most solid can suddenly shift? Meaning cannot be fixed with the walls in play. But K, Jr. had escaped the worst of it, and he had made accommodations for the next time, readying the walls for the patching compound and the new coat of paint, bolting the bookcases to the studs with tri-weight screws, securing the cabinets and the doors. Now he was safe. Normalcy returned. Dinnertime in the park. The homeless ate soup. K, Jr. waited for the next aftershock, intent on the cracks lacing the walls of his home.

He spent a few minutes resetting the clocks, restoring the time on the VCR which flashed 12:00 in blue numerals. And he found many new cracks on the walls on his apartment, new cracks over the doors, new cracks in the walls, deeper indentions developing in the existing cracks, a widening and a separation, the plaster board crumbling into a crushed mix of plaster and paint and pressed gypsum that collected along the baseboard and in the rug. The outside did not show through but some of the holes were big enough to admit small animals.

K, Jr. had purchased several cheap plants to cover the holes until the landlord could make repairs. K, Jr. either forgot them and under-watered or, realizing that he had forgotten, nearly drowned them with too much attention; the plants were in bad shape with yellow places on the leaves where there should have been green, brown stems, mud in place of moist earth.

He took the trash out back to the dumpster. A car pulled up in the alley between buildings. It was far too dark to see face of the driver, only the glowing tip of a cigarette visible. The driver honked his horn several times. K, Jr. threw the sacks of trash on top of the dumpster. The driver honked again. No one responded. For the next fifteen minutes the driver kept honking. Then there was the sound of an engine racing, tires squealing, dirt being thrown on the pavement and one long, sustained blast on the horn.

The clocks were flashing again, the VCR offering 12:00, 12:00, 12:00. Again K, Jr. reset the clocks, restored the VCR. He had to go back and forth quickly from the bedroom to the kitchen so that both clocks showed the proper time.

He washed his face, changed his clothing, put on a heavy sweater and went to meet his girlfriend, Ramona, for dinner. There were plenty of parking spaces on the street. All of the shop windows were boarded up and none of them open except for one Thai restaurant. But with the exception of a single waiter, a woman behind a counter working on a cross-word puzzle, and what sounded like the cooks talking in the back, there was no one else there.

Ramona kept him waiting for twenty minutes. He spent the time drumming on the table with chopsticks, drumming on a ceramic vase holding artificial flowers, drumming on his leg. The waiter made several trips by and kept asking, "You ready to order now? You ready to order now?"

Then she arrived with a bedraggled man who kept staring at the floor. "You remember Samuel don't you?," she said.

Samuel her ex-husband. Samuel a once small but lean man who used to run ultra-marathons. The transformation from the man whose picture was still in a small frame Ramona kept on a shelf in her apartment and this one was astonishing. It was as if someone had stolen his body and replaced it with a limp, submissive wraith.

"I think you two have met," she said. "Didn't you once meet? After our divorce? His house was destroyed. He has nowhere to stay."

This meant her ex-husband was now staying with her? K, Jr. did not say this aloud, just then. He had to press his fingertips to his lips to stay silent. Ramona had a weakness for men she thought she could rehabilitate, like annual remodeling projects. The waiter handed out menus. The entire glass front of the restaurant was boarded up, closing the room from the street, except for a strip of glass at the bottom of the door that had miraculously escaped breakage, making a long and narrow room exceedingly narrow with the outside unavailable. K, Jr. took several hurried sips of water.

The waiter told them that most of the items on the menu were, unfortunately, not available that night, and that the refrigerators were still out, but that they appreciated the business during this very difficult time.

"Maybe we should try somewhere else," K, Jr. said and placed his menu on the table.

"We can't just run out on them," Ramona said. She picked the menu up and handed it back to him, thrust it at him. "Not during this very difficult time. I appreciate the fact that they've remained open during this very difficult time. So many places have given up, without a fight. Thrown in the towel, gone down silently. These people have the true American entrepreneurial spirit. Besides, I like this restaurant. I've always liked this restaurant. Bring us what you can," she told the waiter. "Where's your spirit of adventure?"

Where was his spirit of adventure, indeed, as the waiter returned in twenty minutes with bowls full of mushy white rice, a thin, yellowish soup with strips of green onions floating on the surface, and cups of lukewarm tea. The waiter set this down in front of each of them and said, "So sorry, still no gas in kitchen. We make in microwave. Special discount for you."

"That's so nice of you," Ramona said. "Isn't that nice? That's really nice. It is. You can be sure we'll be back," she told the waiter.

Samuel said nothing. He took little sips of soup. Small bites of rice. He seemed barely with them in the room, his eyes focused on his plate. When he looked up, he chose to stare at a spot on the wall six feet above and between K, Jr.'s and Ramona's heads. He turned his head between bites and surveyed the plywood at the front of the room. "Good board up," he said.

K, Jr. waited for something else, waited for a better explanation from Ramona. They kept on eating. He managed small sips of tea, small bites a rice, some of the soup. He vowed to call out for pizza as soon as he got home.

Ramona said, "Samuel is going to be working for a company that's helping resettle people displaced by the earthquake."

"Where will they be resettling them?" said K, Jr.

Samuel said nothing. He worked on his soup, stared at the table, brought the spoon to his mouth, to the bowl, back to his mouth. He slurped.

"They've hired him for his negotiating skills. I think it's wonderful."

"He'll be talking to people, on behalf of the displaced?"

"Talking and negotiating and helping. All the things Samuel does best. Wonderful. It's just wonderful. It's the American entrepreneurial spirit at work. Through Samuel. I'd say this earthquake is about the most wonderful that's happened to this city."

"Ahead of the mudslides and the fires and the riots? Or would you say it's in the middle of that list," said K, Jr.

Ramona brought her spoon down to her plate. "Your problem is you always see the glass half-empty," she said. "Do you know that? This is a wonderful opportunity. Anyone who sees it as anything else isn't worth speaking to. People are coming together. People like Samuel are getting an opportunity to do good for others. This is how we heal. This city is a living, breathing organism that has been damaged, and now it's going to get better. I'm glad to be a part of that. Through Samuel."

"Water," said Samuel.

"Of course. Of course." She poured for him. "The triumph of will is what's on display here, people's mastery over adversity. You see it on every street corner. You're seeing it in this restaurant tonight. No stoves. No refrigerator. Do you think that stops them? Absolutely not. They put out an entirely wonderful, nourishing meal, and they did it with American ingenuity. The microwave. I never would have thought of that. Well, Samuel would have. And you might have, too, if you weren't so intent on looking at things with the lights out. It's bright out there, and wonderful. Samuel is a part of that and I am proud of him for being a part of that. Someone who's going to be with me should be aware of this. It's what I'd want in a life partner. And what are you doing? What role are you playing? These are rhetorical questions, but you need to think about these things. You really do."

"Smoke," Samuel said. He stood up and wandered off toward the back, behind the counter.

"Is he all right?" K, Jr. said.

Ramona waved her hand, waved off the question. There were shouts from the back, the clatter of pans dropping, Samuel drifted back in their direction, and went out the front door.

"What, exactly, are you hoping to do for him?"

"I told you, his place was destroyed. The whole block condemned. He's lucky he's wasn't killed. He escaped with a few scratches, and the clothes on his back. It was terribly dramatic."

"Is he seeing anyone about this?"

"I was the first one he came too, at 5 AM, he came to my door. It was wonderful and terrible. Poor Samuel."

K, Jr. could see Samuel's legs through the door. He was standing between parked cars with his back toward them. K, Jr. couldn't tell what he was doing. He said, "Is this part of your desire for adventure? You didn't used to take in strays."

"This is not about you."

"Why don't you stay with me and let him stay by himself in your apartment. I'd be much more comfortable with that arrangement."

"How sweet of you. You haven't said anything like that to me in a long me. Now, now. Jealousy is unbecoming. We have to help each other in times like this. That's just what I was talking about before. Triumph. Will. Adversity."

"Samuel."

"Yes, Samuel."

"Aren't you the Ramona who described her divorce as a midnight showing of 'Hell on Earth' that never ended, who said that men are only worthy of castration, and told me that the whole process was so acrimonious that if you'd had a gun—and you said this on more than one occasion—that if you'd had a gun you would have gut-shot Samuel and taken your chances with a jury?"

"Did I say that?" Ramona said and giggled. "I feel like I'm drunk on this tea." She held up her cup. "T-E-A. If you mix up the letters it's E-A-T. It could also be A-E-T. I guess that doesn't spell anything, does it. A fraternity maybe. A sorority. Whoo. Whee. It's good tea. Do you like it? I like it. I like this place. Samuel does too. I can tell."

"You were very specific about the details."

"Cheers," she said.

"Very specific. So specific that I sometimes wake up with bad dreams about it."

"Okay. I was exaggerating. Can't you see that? Certainly I was. I believe in the institution of marriage. But back then, I wanted you and everyone to feel sorry for me. I was at the lowest point on the cycle of self-esteem. You know I'm feeling much better about myself. That's why I can stand back and objectively see what a wreck I was back then. Do you honestly think I could shoot anyone? Especially Samuel. Look at him. He's hardly a threat. He's so broken by this experience. He needs my help. He needs the salvation of human compassion and I intend to reach out to him."

Against all better judgment, against all advice, against all common sense, against everything he had learned about women, K, Jr. said: "Where is he sleeping?"

"Well, my apartment is small."

"That's why I asked. My apartment is much larger. Plenty of room for you."

"All right. We have been sleeping in the same bed. But nothing is happening. It's a convenience. We do it because there's only one bed. But we're past the physical part of things, way past."

She cast her eyes down to the table for a moment and said, "I have to be truthful and I guess that's not entirely the truth. When Samuel came over I was so glad to be alive that I needed the comfort of a human body. We took comfort in each other. Just that once."

"Where was I when this was going on?"

"Yes. Where were you?"

"You could have taken comfort with me. I'm available to comfort you."

"It only happened once. I told you. It hasn't happened again. We don't do it anymore. This was a matter of comfort. Human comfort. You can understand that, can't you?"

"I hope you'll be as understanding if the shoe changes feet."

"I'll kill you. That's exactly what broke Samuel and me up in the first place. This was comfort. I needed to be held. You weren't around. Where were you when I needed you? The sex, well, it just happened. I'll kill you. Don't ever. Don't even think."

She folded her hands across her chest and turned away from him. There was not much left to the dinner after that. K, Jr. had no appetite. The music in the restaurant was too loud, and it seemed as if "Love Is Blue" (performed by Paul Marrat) played over and over again. K, Jr. was sure of it and asked the Thai waiter. There was hasty conference in the corner, and the music changed.

"So sorry," the waiter said. "Button stuck on repeat."

"I was wondering," K, Jr. said.

"Not crazy. Care for desert now?"

Ramona and Samuel said goodbye to K, Jr. on the sidewalk. The division was clear. The two of them stood together on one side of a square of cracked pavement, K, Jr. stood on the other.

Ramona said, "I'm going to be very busy for the next couple of days, maybe the whole next week. Samuel really needs my help. You understand."

Samuel dug his toe into the sidewalk, examining the gutter for—prizes? She took him by the arm and they walked away.

"I was in the earthquake too," K, Jr. said.

His hands flung from his body, the stiff neck, hunched shoulders, cant of the left foot inward, hands raised, palms slicing in a fending gesture. He tilted north.

"You're much stronger," Ramona called, still walking away. "You can manage without me.

Though you won't admit it, you have the spirit of adventure. It's why I stay with you. I'll call you soon."

Samuel leaned on her as if he were drunk. They were a full block away when Samuel turned around for a moment and smiled the broadest, widest, knowingest grin K., Jr. had ever seen. Then he leaned back into Ramona, his step a bit springier.

"He's so tired," she shouted. "This is difficult."

"That fucker," said K, Jr., and that was just the problem: it hadn't been difficult at all. He'd been snaked. There was no defense. If he'd had something of hers right then he would have thrown it on the ground. How pitiful that would have been.

K, Jr. tried the burners on his stove. Still no gas, and thus no heat, no hot water. He called four pizza places. No one was delivering. He heated two cans of soup in his microwave and ate them. He had a half-filled pint of ice cream in the freezer. He ate that. He found some nuts in a bottle on a shelf way in back. He ate that. He found a package of marshmallows left over from a camping trip. The top third were moldy but the ones on the bottom seemed fine. He broke open the food in his earthquake emergency pack. There was enough for three days. He ate it all. This was no time to worry about cholesterol.

He filled a plastic container with water and put it in the microwave. While it was running, he undressed. He was beginning to develop an excess of flesh along around his waist. He ate anything that was in front of him, his hand moving to his mouth compulsively. Someone needed to stop him. He needed to stop himself.

He came into the kitchen with a towel around him, carried the plastic container into the bath, ran the water, used a washcloth combining the tap water with the heated water from the container. His control of temperature was an inexact science. He froze or he burned. He supposed he was clean enough.

At 3 AM another aftershock swept through the building. The frame shivered, the joints creaking low like sacks of earth being moved. A door banged. The bed rocked, left and right and back again. K, Jr. came awake quickly at the start of the first rumbling. He lay there trying to decide if this were the real thing necessitating his getting out of bed and taking cover under the doorway, or if could he ride it out in bed. Before he decided, it ended. But there was banging from the kitchen, and the motion sensors in the main room went off.

K, Jr. struggled out of bed, put on a robe, went into the living room and shut off the alarm. The pipes screamed overhead, the old woman in 4B was bathing again. 3 AM her favored time for an investigation of dirt, oblivious to the water spilling out of her tub. She never answered the door. He inspected his apartment but there was no sign of a break-in that had been foiled by the alarm. Then he found a single plate that had been flipped out of the cabinet, landing face down on the floor. The motion of the door opening, the plate flying, set off the alarm.

He was about to shut off the lights, about to return to bed, another aftershock. He caught a plate coming out of the cabinet. A crack in the wall developed as he watched. Afterward, he put a quilt around himself and went out on the patio. He held the neighbor's cat in his lap, stroking it until it became light.

II.

THE BLUE CURTAIN HAD MOVED again, covering two of the four entrances to the building. A line of cars waited to get into The Complex's parking structure, down the concrete ramp, through the gates. When it was K, Jr.'s turn, he pulled in and followed the orange signs down and around and around and down to a part of the parking structure he'd never seen before.

The strange breeze that had no known origin continued to blow, but cold and wet now, as if its source had changed from the desert to the coast. The floor was damp and slimy in places. Vertical cracks defaced all of the walls. The floor was the raw gray of unfinished concrete, unpainted, not lined for parking spaces. Cars had pulled in at odd angles as the drivers attempted to claim some kind of open area for themselves. K, Jr. parked next to a wall, under a broad metal beam.

There were no elevators, only a narrow dark staircase which he followed up five flights. The staircase deposited him in a corridor which was filled with debris. In places, acoustic tile hung from the ceiling. In others, the tiles had fallen or had been forcibly removed, littering the floor with two-foot squares, leaving the sprinkler piping, red and blue and yellow electrical wires, silver air-conditioning ducts and black computer lines visible. K, Jr. moved slowly down the hall, a hall he was sure he had never seen before. Nor had he been in this building, or known of its existence, couldn't tell who used to work here, if the wreckage was deliberate or a consequence of the earthquake and its aftershocks.

He moved into a larger area that appeared to have been rapidly abandoned, as if before an attacking army. Papers littered the floor, dictionaries and secretarial handbooks strewn among them, television monitors lay on their sides, typewriters flipped over and smashed on the ground, computers open and cannibalized, high-backed chairs broken and flung about. Office doors, torn from their hinges, balanced on desks. Stuffing had been pulled from the sofas and thrown. Glass was broken, the lighting sporadic: some of the fluorescents pulsed at uneven intervals. In the corners, the wall coverings had pulled away from the walls. Wallpaper hung in strips. There were puddles on the floor, the carpeting stank of must and mildew and rot.

He went past an office where someone used a crowbar to destroy everything inside. There was a tremendous crash as the man threw his chair through the hermetically sealed window then started hurling the contents of the office outside. He flipped the desk over a couple of time, got it up on one end, then dropped it out the window. "That's better," he said. "Now I finally have some room to work in."

Christian was in one of the offices, clutching a seat cushion to his chest. "We've been reassigned," he said.

His walls were lined with autographed pictures declaring Christian a best friend, the glass fronts shattered. A few jagged pieces of glass stayed in the frames, the rest fallen. Two large banana plants stood in the corners, the leaves stripped from the trunk creating two whip thin green rods pointing toward the ceiling. His desk was empty but the floor was covered with papers as if giant hands had collected them in a bundle from the top of the desk and thrown them into the air to settle where they might.

"Reassigned."

"To what?" said K, Jr.

"It's worse than I thought. Slaughter doesn't even describe it. Everyone from VP and above has been let go. That's one of the rumors."

"Is it true?"

"All rumors are true. The bank may intercede. Federal troops might be called in."

"Do you know anything, really? We need to find out who to report to and what we're supposed to do."

"The phones are down. All lines of communications in and out have been severed."

"Christian."

"That's another rumor."

"And the memo?"

"Yes. All of it. Reassigned."

"Do you know what we're supposed to do?"

Christian shook his head. "I know you didn't have any part of this. Columns five and six were not mentioned in the report. What do you think that means?"

"What did McPursky say?"

"Who is McPursky?"

"What do you mean, 'who is McPursky?' What did he say?"

Christian rocked in his chair. "We're to wait for instructions. Your office is down the hall. It's in bad shape. Steel yourself."

"Yes, but what did McPursky say?"

"There is no McPursky. Now we wait."

"There has to be some recourse here. Where are all my things? They can't just move us like us this. Where are we? We have to make a formal protest."

"No protests. Protests are a mistake. Mistakes can't be abided. Haven't you learned that by now?"

"Christian, I'm not going to accept this kind of treatment. After what the whole city has been through it's cruel, horribly cruel to subject anyone to this kind of additional stress. We shouldn't even be working. I intend to protest."

"No. No. Don't do it. Please. I could be affected by this."

"I won't bring up your name. Besides it has nothing to do with you specifically. I'm the one who'll be protesting."

"I could be affected," Christian said. "Those of us who are left. Don't do it. We have to pull together." He suddenly leaned over and began picking up papers, putting them on the desk. Some of them fell off the top of the pile, back to the floor. "We'll work on the report. They'll understand."

K, Jr. left Christian rocking in his chair, sorting papers, still claiming, "They would understand." He went farther down the hall. The three men from Maintenance were walking by. One of them carried a shovel. One of them carried a box. The third carried a small square of glass wrapped in paper. They dressed in black jumpsuits and all three wore wide black back-support belts, like old-time corsets encircling their waists, connected to shoulder straps as well.

"I've heard I'm going to need some help with my office," K, Jr. said.

"Hay un reporte y lo investigaramos."

"What are you saying?"

"Un reporte. Un reporte."

"A report." That much he understood. "Yes, how long will it take?"

The man with the ladder shrugged. He said something that K, Jr. didn't catch.

"Perdoné la molestia." They walked off.

Three white flowers lay on the carpet behind them. Carnations in full bloom, petals delicately twisted in the heat. K, Jr. left the flowers alone, stepped around them, pretended they were not there.

He circled the floor twice and found no indication of an assigned space. Christian's had his name marked on the outside, the usual plastic name plate in black, block letters. When K, Jr. went back to ask him about the location of his office, Christian was gone, many papers still on the floor, some of them on the desk.

K, Jr. walked past an office in better shape than most. The ceiling tiles were in place, and though the walls were bare, they were unmarked. A leather executive chair behind the desk, a phone on the floor.

The phone rang, continued ringing. K, Jr. felt compelled to answer. A voice said, "Who is this?"

"This is K. And who is this?"

"You're not the usual man. Are you new?"

"The phone was ringing. I picked it up. No one was around."

"It's good you did. The voice mail system isn't functioning right now. That damned new software has a bug in it or something. You'd think with all we spent on the system it would work. But it doesn't. Hangs up when the wrong combination of numbers gets pressed or too many messages try to get taken simultaneously or some damned thing. Say, have we met before?"

"I don't know who you are."

"Well, that's all right. I don't know who you are either. Leave a message and say that I called. Appreciate it."

Before K, Jr. could respond the line went dead. Then another line rang. It was Ramona.

"How did you find me?" K, Jr. said.

"I need to see you tonight."

"What number did you call? Did you call the main number?"

"I know you're upset about Samuel and I want to work things out."

"I know that but I have to know. What did they tell you? Things are...peculiar here. There's a lot of uncertainty."

"Uncertainty is part of life," Ramona said. "The only thing that is certain is that we're going to die. We live and we die. That much we know. Except we don't know when. That was a very important part of my self-esteem retraining. Acceptance. Renewal. It's liberating. It's allows you to simply—"

"Ramona. Ramona. What number did you call?"

"I'm beginning to notice a pattern here. You don't seem terribly interested in my self-esteem."

"I'm very interested in your self-esteem. Your self-esteem is the source of my self-esteem. I've heard what you said and I believe we're all part of a collective self-esteem."

"What are wonderful insight. I knew there was depth to you. You just hide it."

"Please. What number did you call?"

"When I called back in on the main number they transferred me to you."

"I can see you tonight. What time?"

"There was some confusion, though. It rang one place and no one had ever heard of you. Have you been lying to me all this time? Do you really work there? That's another thing that broke Samuel and me up. He told me he was an important businessman but he was really just a clerk."

"You know my usual schedule," he said.

"I'm concerned about you. Are you telling me the truth? Truth is the most important thing."

"You were married to him for five years and you didn't know what he did?"

"Do any of us ever really know what we do? The important thing is the truth and the honesty. I have to be with a man of action and integrity. Is that you?"

"I can meet you anytime after 6."

"The truth about a lot of people is coming out. You've seen how well Samuel is adjusting to his circumstances. What spirit! What *jouissance*."

"Yes. I've seen," said K, Jr.. I should go home first. Clean up. I'm still cleaning up."

"I'd hate it if both you and Samuel were out of a job."

"I'm not out of a job."

Christian went running by. He waved and held a fist up to his ear to indicate that K, Jr. should call when he was free. "Christian," he said. "Christian. Wait a minute, please."

Ramona said, "And you are what you say you are?"

"I think I have to go."

"Are you really what you say you are?"

"I'm exactly what I've told you I am," said K, Jr. "No more and no less. I'm your little Fima."

"Don't say that. Not over the phone. God, if anyone heard. Only in bed, I'd die if anyone knew."

"No one can hear us."

"What if they can?"

"I appreciate that. Samuel and you, well it's making me uncomfortable. I know you said nothing's going on but you slipped once…"

"Let's meet at nine. I'll come over. Have a light dinner first. There's lots to talk about."

"There is?"

"There always is. I'll see you later."

There were no more phone calls, no mail delivery, no one walking past. K, Jr. went to look for Christian, but he was not in his office. K, Jr. went around to the open offices on the floor and began to scavenge, taking furniture, plants, pens, pencils, a desk blotter, paperclips, staple remover, a roll of tape. He removed his jacket and his tie, dragged a desk in from the hall.

He was sweating, still putting things away, ordering the top of his desk, orienting items properly with the angle of the wall and the shadow of the overhead lighting, when a man carrying a clipboard entered the office. "I see you're all set up," the man said.

"Who told you I was here?"

"Told me? You're on the list," the man said. He wore a white shirt, a red-patterned tie, and he sat down peremptorily in the chair across from K, Jr.'s desk. He made a notation on the top sheet and said, "I wanted to talk to you about possible stress reactions from the earthquake and especially from all of the aftershocks that have been happening. This won't take long."

K, Jr. sat down, too, and said, "Very well."

"It's required. It's a service of The Complex to help in the adjustment. You might be a little more enthusiastic."

"Please. Go ahead. I'm sure this will be very helpful."

"All right then. Number 1. Whether or not they sleep through an earthquake, children may experience anxiety from it. Number 2. Watching television or hearing adults talk about the quake can trigger this anxiety. Number 3. Following a quake, children may become more active or restless, easily upset or withdrawn. Number 4—"

"Why are you telling me this?"

"Please, there are quite few on the list and it will go much quicker if you just listen and ask questions at the end. Number 5. I mean Number 4. They have to come in order. Number 4. Many children are afraid of sleeping or taking a shower for fear another quake will hit. Number 5. Some worry about what will happen to them if their homes have been damaged and what has happened to their lost pets. Number 6. Help children feel safe by allowing them to talk about it. Avoid the temptation to say, 'Don't worry, everything will be fine.' It's important that their fears come to the surface and are treated as legitimate."

"Excuse me."

"Please. Only a few more. Number 7. It's important for parents to control their emotions in front of their children. If parents can handle a quake, it's likely that their kids will also. Number 8. Give your children factual information about the earthquake. Explain calmly and matter-of-factly where the event took place and how close it was so your children don't have a heightened sense of anxiety. Number 9. Children typically have separation anxiety under these circumstances. It's important to assure them that, should you be separated, you have a plan as to how to get to them. Remind them that the school has a disaster preparedness plan and that they will be safe until you come for them. Number 10. Maintain your child's routine as much as possible, as there is a sense of safety in routine. Number 11. If all this fails, don't hesitate to seek professional help. That's my list. I have extra copies if you'd like to have one to study. I hope this information will be of some use to you."

"But I have no children," said K, Jr.

The man flushed deeply and said, "But there must be some mistake." He flipped back and forth from paper to paper examining the columns. He said, "My list says you have children."

"I haven't any."

"The list is never wrong. Are you sure you have no children? Denial is one of the reactions from this kind of stress. You were at the meeting about adult reactions. You should know what to be prepared for."

"I was at no such meeting. I never heard about any meeting. When was this?"

"How long have you been with the company?" the man said. "How long have you worked here at The Complex? There was a memo. Everyone was there. My list says you were there."

"I wasn't there and I don't have any children. But if I get any you'll be the first one I tell. You can be there to witness the birth, if you wish. I could consider you as one of the possible candidates for godfather. Of course, first I'm going to have to find a woman willing to bear my children. As of now, I don't seem terribly close to such an outcome. Maybe you know someone you can introduce me to? Do you have a sister?"

"Now, just a moment. Just one minute. There is nothing to be making jokes about. The list says you have children, a boy and a girl, and so you must. I have it right here. Mr. John Kaye. K-A-Y-E."

"That isn't me. That's not how my name is spelled. My first name isn't John."

"Well you could have told me. Saved me a lot of time wasted." He stood up abruptly and tipped over his chair. "You see. The list isn't wrong. Mr. John Kaye does have children. Even if that isn't you."

"You asked me if my name was K and I told you. You've only wasted your own time and mine. With all these mistakes it begins to make me wonder if I should trust anything you're saying. All of this good advice of yours. Why should I believe any of it?"

"I intend to report this. It's just the kind of attitude we can't have at a time like this. Expect there to be repercussions, sir. Good day." He strode out of the office and huffed up the hallway, accompanying himself with mutterings which died out as he moved farther and farther away.

K, Jr. went off to the bathroom. He splashed water on his face, the water slipped through his fingers, massaged his temples and forehead vigorously. He stretched toward the ceiling, swung his hips, arched then cracked his back, did deep knee-bends, bent his leg up at knee, grabbed his toe and stretched his thigh muscles, touched his toes, did jumping jacks, ran in place. The lights went out.

K, Jr. had to feel his way to the door, the darkness maintained by a set of two doorways that sealed any trace of the outside insuring complete privacy and total tomb-like black. He bumped into a tiled wall and kicked over a wastebasket before he was able to get back to the hall.

All the lights were out on the floor. A voice on the overhead speaker said, "This is building security. This is building security. Attention. Attention. This is building security."

K, Jr. waited for the rest of the message, for information on the lights. Nothing more was said.

Despite the darkness, he saw a team of men suspended from a platform on the exterior of his new office. They were bricking up the window from the outside. It was a fascinatingly simple operation: bricks tapped into place, a layer of mortar, more bricks. They had half the window finished. K, Jr. stood and banged on the glass, shouting, "What are you doing?"

They waved back and the work proceeded quickly, bricks and a layer of mortar and more bricks, rising up the glass, closing out the window and the light. K, Jr. immediately picked up the phone to call offices services but the extension had been changed. "I can't help you," the person at the other end said. "I'm new here." He tried security and got purchasing. He tried payroll and got reprographics. He tried parking and got taxes. He tried audio visual and got corporate services. He tried file storage and got a fax number. He tried insurance and got labor relations. He tried life safety and the phone rang and rang and rang before someone picked up then hung up immediately without saying anything. He tried finance and got recycling. Then he called the sequence again and got voice mail every time telling him to leave a message and someone would call him back, thank you.

He ran back to Christian's office but there was still no sign of his associate. When he returned to his office the lights in the building came on at that exact moment making his reflection available in the glass, the bricks beyond, drying into place. His computer lumbered to life with a series of beeps, the printer rolled and ground into readiness. The monitor requested his password. K, Jr. typed in the usual and was rejected. Three times he tried, three times he was rejected. Then the monitor displayed the error message, "Invalid password. System disengaged from Lan Ceom-24. User lockout. Contact your network administrator." Then the display on the front of the printer began flashing "Me Feed Envelope." K, Jr. shut it off.

No computer, no window, no phones, K, Jr. went down to the commons area for lunch. As he approached, one by one the windows of the food concessions slammed shut. He knocked on the window and said, "It isn't two o'clock yet."

"Closing time," someone said from behind the metal screen.

"Your watch is fast. You can't tell me all the food is gone."

"Closing time. Come back tomorrow."

"Can't you make an exception?"

"Go away. We're closed. We're closed."

The only other shops in the area were a dry cleaners, a shipping and packaging shop, a jewelry store and a barber. A counter person stood ready in each but they were otherwise empty.

The employee lounge was similarly deserted. The change machine was out of order, something K, Jr. didn't discover until he had tried three dollars and received nothing in return. He slapped the machine in frustration but quickly decided that perhaps that was all right—the only choices the vending machine offered were bean burritos, extra spicy. Each one of the selections in the drink machine flashed "OUT." The shelves of the candy machine were empty, the ice cream machine turned off. The coffee machine had a sign saying, Out of Order.

K, Jr.'s office door was locked and he had no key. He knew he had left it open—for just that reason. There was mail lying on the ground in front of the door in the shape of a cross. No, in the shape of a T, the shape of a T. He was certain he saw the T.

He heard the sound of a cart rolling and ran up the hall. He saw the mail boy disappearing around the corner, ran faster, saw him around another corner, another corner, at the far end of the hall. K, Jr. ran but couldn't get closer. When he reached the lobby, the elevator doors were just closing.

All of the office doors were locked, including Christian's. He pounded on Christian's door but received no answer. He sat in one of the cubicles. The telephone worked but he didn't know who to call.

The three men from Maintenance came down the hall. One of them carried a pair of bolt cutters, one of them carried a roll of wire, the third had a crystal vase. They were in blue jumpsuits, the white patch over their hearts still blank.

K, Jr. stood up and confronted them. He said, "My office is locked. Can you open the door?"

There was a quick conference and then the man with the bolt cutters said, "*Hay un reporte y lo investigaramos.*"

"Don't tell me that. If you're asking me to fill out some report, I'm not going to do it. N. O. Forget about a report. You never answer them and I'm through wasting my time. And don't give me any Spanish about how busy you are. I don't care how busy you are. I don't care anything. You will open my door, right now."

The three men stood in the hallway but did nothing. K, Jr. panted from yelling. After a few more seconds of unresponsiveness, he picked up the telephone from his cubicle and threw it at their feet where it smashed, the receiver bouncing off the wall, the electronics hanging out. The man with the bolt cutters retrieved the damaged phone, held it at his waist.

K, Jr. pounded vigorously on his door then pointed to the lock. "My door," he said. "Now."

"*Sí. Sí.*" He pulled out a single key, examined some impossibly small markings, then opened up the door to K, Jr.'s new office.

"I'm glad we understand each other," K, Jr. said. "I wouldn't want this to happen again. We won't speak of it. There are too many mistakes being made at this company where everyone says no one makes mistakes."

"*Perdoné la molestia*," the man with the bolt cutters said.

"Now I'll need that key so we won't have this problem again." K, Jr. held out his hand.

"Don't say anything. I don't care if you can't understand. Give me the key."

The key was handed over. The men from Maintenance continued down the hall.

A medal of St. Christopher hung from the handle of his door. He grabbed it and threw it down the hall though it didn't go very far. He ran down the hall and threw it again, the medal landing with a clatter somewhere on something hard.

K, Jr. considered going home. Who would know? But the lure of his paycheck was strong, the responsibility of rent, car payment, three kinds of insurance, and a Christmas account stronger still. He spent the rest of the afternoon constructing a guide to the phone system. He was not able to reach the MIS Department or Office Services or Building Management or Central Distribution though he asked everyone he called if they knew the extension. He was told to look in the directory and he said those numbers didn't work. He was told that he must be mistaken. All the numbers worked. How could the numbers not work? After that, he said he had no directory, it had been lost as a result of earthquake damage. He received sympathy for his loss, but no one could help him still.

There was a pile of folders waiting for him when he returned from another trip to the men room. No mail boy, just the files stacked neatly in the center of his desk, tabs toward the window. He put them on the floor. Without a computer there was nothing to be done with them. Without direction from his immediate superior there was nothing to be done with them.

At precisely 6 o'clock he set the phone on forward, pushed in his chair, put his suit coat on, picked up his briefcase and went to the parking structure.

People were still driving poorly on the way home, ignoring lights, not signaling, hoping to stretch yellows through crowded intersection. K, Jr. pulled over and waited for a half-hour for the traffic to die down, for some semblance of calm to descend on the streets.

The hot water had returned but still no heat. K, Jr. took a sponge bath. He remained uneasy about the shower, afraid to be caught if another quake, or aftershock came.

The pizza stores were delivering, the only restaurants answering their phones. K, Jr. ordered two large plain ones. They arrived cold but he didn't care, eating in fast bites, half a slice at a time, ripping off the crusts, keeping his mouth full.

Ramona didn't call, and the nine o'clock date passed. He tried her phone without an answer. He watched a little bit of television but grew tired of seeing the same stories of the newly homeless, the loss, the human misery, all of it gleefully recorded by reporters who affected tones of sorrow and consolation but whose job was to leech off the suffering of others. Just tell me how you feel.

Ramona arrived close to midnight. At the door K, Jr. told her, "This is awfully late."

She laughed, threw back her head and laughed, turned her head to the side and laughed, tilted downward and laughed. The bones of her face had eroded, ridging her skin into red waves without chin. No angles for the eye to behold. K, Jr. heard of a wood-frame building that went down in three seconds. Unbolted, it was lifted off the foundation, returned to the earth, the second floor smashing through to ground level. Then there was a darkness greater than any known darkness. She smiled and said it was his job to service her. Lateral stresses overwhelmed vertical loads. No one made it alive, trapped in their beds, compressed into linen, crushed in the space of a sigh. Tonight. Tonight, give it to her good. The trembling merged with the rush of the earth, the known separating out from certainty. Interior walls vanished. She wore her red underwear as an enticement. He didn't know anyone who lived there. Fire could burn through water. Smoke always obscured, this step might be the right one. This step might pitch us through a hole. She lifted away her blouse. It was another tan building on a street of tan buildings across from a park—but there was easy access for the news. She thought it was a secret, underneath. Land was not land, only a larger column of dirt piled high. Her lace frayed along the shoulder, the cups didn't fit. Such a fragile thing, plywood, and how could we trust doorframes to bear the weight for whole structures? She was smooth and flat all the way down, so white, she had little contrast with her background. The search went on for the bodies. They brought in the dogs. They measured distances in inches now, calculating known air. Eventually, no one could breathe. He ignored her open arms. "What about Samuel?" he said.

"I want you."

He ignored the thrust of her pelvis, her insistence on the couch.

"Why now?"

"It's how I feel."

There was an aftershock. He waited for the building to steady, a move to a new equilibrium. Two cracks appeared above the door.

"Is it that you're not interested—or you can't?" Ramona said.

"There are too many distractions," he said beginning to envision a world without her. What would he give up without the closure of her arms?

"It's the stress," she said. "Perfectly normal. Let me try some things on you."

"Ramona."

"Wicked things."

K, Jr. said no and she pouted for a few minutes. "You could at least try," she said.

"Isn't Samuel waiting for you at home?"

"Someone is waiting for me. At home. Someone who tries. You're losing your spirit of adventure. That's a bad sign," Ramona said.

Only a few minutes after she left K, Jr. was motivated to do something, anything. A gesture, a word. Something other than smoke. He gathered up two blankets he never used, six cans of soup, two rolls of toilet paper, and placed them in a paper shopping bag. Newly homeless camped across the street in one of the ten tent cities. The usually homeless mingled with the newly so; everyone smelled.

He locked his door and walked across the street. A sheet of plastic fencing ran across the center. On one side, the National Guard administered the tents. Green affairs, lines taut, tightly pegged to the ground, no blousing to the sides. Six tents by six tents in excellent symmetry. K, Jr. believed if he measured he would discover the identical distance between tents, proscribed by the government books written about such things.

He came up to the breech in the fence, a soldier stood guard. "May I help you, sir?" the soldier said.

K, Jr. offered the bag. The guard peered inside and said, "That's very nice of you, sir. But it needs to go to the disbursement center."

"Couldn't you just take it. Give it to someone who might need it. It's extra. I went through my things. I wanted to do something. I've been watching the news."

"The disbursement center is open between nine and four. It's at the other end of the compound."

"You can't just take it? How about if I leave it here and you pretend that it just showed up. Some things for people less fortunate."

"Please come back between those hours, sir. That's what is required."

"Why don't I just hand it out. To someone inside."

"Not possible, sir. This compound is for displaced persons only. Are you displaced?"

K, Jr. considered the question.

"That needs to go to the disbursement center, sir. Those are my orders."

K, Jr. walked up and down the rows of tents on the public side. There was no order here. People had tied pieces of plastic to trees, to the backstop of the softball diamond, to light poles. Poorly rigged affairs, thrown up by those who never camped, who hated camping, who had never thought about camping until the preceding week.

No one wanted his bag with the blankets and the soup and the toilet paper. He carried the bag from tent to tent, walking the entire length of the park.

He went home to his dark house. The soup went back on the shelves, the blankets in the closet, the rolls of toilet paper under the sink. K, Jr. went to bed.

Two hours later there was a tapping on the door, the insistent tapping of someone who didn't realize they were tapping. A reflex. K, Jr. asked who it was but knew, somehow, that it was Christian. He undid the two dead bolts above the door which was itself made of solid core. He opened the door to admit a shivering Christian. Christian transferred his tapping to the doorframe. Tapping, with the tips of his right hand's index and middle fingers, the fingers stiffened, tapping, incessantly tapping.

"No questions," Christian said. "They're too obvious. I was checking up on you. I'm worried. I didn't see you in your office at all this afternoon. I was concerned that you were let go. But your name didn't appear on any of my lists."

"This is late for visitors."

"I had to talk with you. I've been all over The Complex today trying to find out what's going on. I thought your protest letter might have been the cause. It's raised quite a stir."

The tapping, the incessant tapping. K, Jr. reached out and put his hand over Christian's hands. The tapping ceased. "You're going to wear a hole in the wood," he said.

"The update they sent around said that talking was important. We all have to realize that we're not alone. You know you're not alone. Don't you? I didn't lose much. Glass and china. Wedding presents that we never used. My wife flew back east. Until things improve."

"Can we discuss this tomorrow?" K, Jr. said. "At the office? I'm tired."

"We're supposed to talk. It's not only healthy but it helps relieve the pain we're feeling. They said it expedites healing."

"I need to try and sleep. I haven't been sleeping. Another aftershock woke me. I haven't been sleeping at all. I'm not sure I'm awake now. I might be dreaming you."

"Who has. Do you have anything to eat?"

"Come in," said K, Jr.

They settled in the kitchen. K, Jr. pulled out box of the leftover pizza. "Do you want me to warm it?" he said.

"Let's just talk. We need to talk."

K, Jr. set the box on the table. Christian opened it and began eating. His left hand moved to his mouth, back to the box, back to his mouth. He seemed entirely unconscious of his eating, of the movements of his hand as if eating were an act independent of their conversation. Between bites, his right hand tapped. It only stopped when his left was engaged in bringing a slice of pizza to his mouth.

Again K, Jr. covered Christian's hands. "Stop that," he said. "You have to stop that."

"I didn't know."

"Let's talk," K, Jr. said. "Go ahead."

"You first."

"What do you mean me first? You said you had something to say."

"I told you, your protest letter caused quite a stir. I thought you were let go. I was concerned."

"But I never sent it. I thought about what you said and decided to wait until everything settled down."

"They got it. They heard you loud and clear. And the incident with Maintenance. People have been talking about that."

"I needed my door opened. I wasn't willing to wait six months for them to answer my request."

"It was a bold move. You've been noticed."

"And what about the memo? What about our work? Who is in charge now?"

"I was unable to establish that. But I was able to fill out a requisition for office supplies and to get a list of the current working extensions. Of course that's only valid for tomorrow. It may change. Do you have anything else to eat?"

K, Jr. folded the now empty box and threw it in the trash. "I have some soup," he said.

"Soup. That would be good. I like soup."

The tapping. The fingers working on the table top. K, Jr. tried to ignore it. "How important can work be in the face of this?" he said.

"We have to continue. We have to go on."

"You were just telling me the opposite yesterday."

"I've changed."

The microwave beeped to signal it had finished heating. K, Jr. put a bowl down in front of Christian.

"You have power," said Christian. "We don't have power. My wife left. She said she needed to be someplace where the ground was solid. She felt cut off. I think she was weak to leave. We have to continue. We have to go on."

"How important is that? I went out to the park. Have you been there? They're living in tents. A city of homeless."

"They're all Mexicans. Illegals. I'm sure of it." His hand tapped faster. "My wife left. Couldn't stay. She was upset by the whole thing. This is when you learn what people are made of."

"You sound like Ramona."

"Who?"

Christian spoke between mouthfuls. He finished the soup, put the spoon in the bowl, tapped on the side, on the table, on his wrist. He changed hands, his left hand tapped. He tapped on his palm, on any flat surface.

"They're not all Mexicans," K, Jr. said, "or illegals and even if they were so what? They don't suffer differently than we do. I brought blankets and soup. Anything to help. It was a good feeling."

"Illegals. All of them."

"It could have been anyone."

"We have to get back to work. I appreciate that you didn't say anything in your letter about me. About what we talked about. You saved me a lot of aggravation."

"Christian, I have to go to sleep now, and you should too. Are you going to be able to get home all right? Do you want to use the couch? I have an extra blanket."

"No, no. I've stayed too long. Thank you for talking."

K, Jr. didn't sleep. Now he was hungry, and all the pizza, all the soup was gone. But he was too tired to go out to an all-night store. He lay in bed and watched the ceiling. There was an aftershock at 6 AM. The ceiling bowed, flecks of plaster coming down.

III.

THE BLUE CURTAIN HAD MOVED and three of the four entrances to The Complex were blocked by it. K, Jr. drove in, although he was the only one driving in. A steady stream of traffic drove out, cars piled high with file boxes, angry men and women sounding on their horns. Strangers wearing ties. Some cried.

He followed the bright arrows indicating where to park and was led in a wide and winding circle that looped around concrete pillars and orange plastic traffic cones, back and forth across the first level floor to send him out of the building without finding a space. On the street, he came around again and entered the building. This time, he pulled his car into any narrow opening that resembled a space. No attendants jumped out from behind poles to warn him off though he was sure his actions were being recorded on the surveillance system. He waved to one of the cameras, saluted to another, put his thumb to his front teeth at a third.

An open staircase, built in a spiral around a planting of tall palms and spreading ferns, led him to the ground level. He went to his new building and tried the door. It was locked. His access card had no effect either. K, Jr. pushed the call button.

"May I help you, sir?" a voice asked.

"I'm trying to get into the building."

"May I help you, sir?"

"I said, I'm trying to get into the building."

"May I help you, sir?"

"Can't you hear me?" He stood close to the speaker grill and shouted. "I'm trying to get into the building."

"May I help you, sir? May I help you, sir?"

He walked down a curved path to the place referred to as the "commons area" between the six buildings of The Complex. In this plaza, where all paths intersected on their way to and from each building, was a center deck, elevated five steps above the ground, constructed some twenty feet square. Set at each corner were planting beds in the shape of raised brick cylinders built up two feet from the ground, that contained small shrubs and arrangements of purple and yellow perennials. The centerpiece of the deck was a sculpture of a huge pitcher standing fifteen feet high, tilted as if someone poured. The pitcher was also a fountain continuously pouring water into a gray-bottomed wading pool, surrounded by gray tiles. The water was clear and streamed in an endless circuit.

No one ever stayed long out there. Only the ledge of the brick planters was available as seats and that was discouraged. No sitting! K, Jr. came by now and thought about stopping, stayed on the walkways at the base of the steps leading upward, went on to the next building.

He had the same problem at the next four building entrances. He could hear the same voice of the security office, but the man could not hear him. There was no activity in the lobby, no one going in nor out.

At the last building K, Jr. tried the door, tried his security card, tried the call button. The voice again said, "May I help you, sir."

"Can you hear me? I'm trying to get into the building."

"Yes, sir, I can hear you quite clearly. How can I help you?"

"I said I'm trying to get into the building. The door is locked and my security card won't work."

"That is correct."

K, Jr. waited for some additional explanation. He was reflected in the glass door. His tie was askew, his collar unbuttoned.

"I have to get into the building."

The voice said, "You are not authorized to enter this building, sir."

"What building am I authorized to enter?"

"I don't have that information sir, I'm sorry."

"Let me speak to your supervisor."

"I am the supervisor."

"You must have a superior. I'll need to speak with him."

"I'm sorry, sir, I'm not authorized to give out that kind of information."

"What is your name?"

"I'm sorry, sir. Company policy does not permit me to give out that information."

"Are you enjoying this?"

"I have no opinion," the voice said.

K, Jr. went back across the courtyard, past the fountain, back to his building. None of them were his building, anymore. He went back to the one where he believed he had left his office the day before. The three men from Maintenance were coming out. They wore beige jumpsuits, their names printed in the white patches above their hearts. But K, Jr. charged through the door and didn't have time to read.

"No, Señor."

"No entrada."

He ignored them, went to the elevator bank, punched the buttons. All six elevators arrived. He stepped into one, punched the fifth floor. But the elevator only went down, depositing him exactly where he had left his car.

The door opened, a set of green rosary beads on the ground before him. He waited but the elevator did not move. He tried all of the buttons with no result. He stepped off, stepped carefully over the beads, and all six doors closed. What now?

He expected to come home and find the door to his apartment blocked by a blue curtain, the three men from Maintenance camped outside telling him he couldn't go in, or to find the building wrapped in a blue curtain or both ends of the street closed off by the blue curtain—and everywhere, the three men from Maintenance directing traffic, setting traffic cones, blocking the path, forever separating him from his home.

He walked from his apartment to a small bakery a few blocks away. The storefront had been untouched by the earthquake though the stores to the right and left had plywood in place of their glass front windows. Both of them were going out of business and offered special sales.

There was a woman seated outside the bakery with a large white dog leashed at her feet. At K, Jr.'s arrival, the dog lunged, bared its teeth and growled.

"Snappy," she said. "Bad dog. Bad dog." The dog growled, but settled at her feet. "Oh you Snappy. Good dog. That's my Snappy. That's my Snappy. That's my precious Snappy-dog. My Snappy-doggy dog. Mommy loves her Snappy-dog. Yes. She does. She does, she does, she does."

Inside, an elderly couple stood at the counter ordering. They bore a striking resemblance though the woman had more gray hair. They seemed to be leaning in, using one another for balance. Two children (grandchildren?) spun around them.

The old man said, "We'll have the blueberry. Is that right?"

The woman behind the counter held a sheet of waxed paper in her hand, ready to pluck the pastries from trays in the display case. The old man turned to his wife. "Blueberry?"

"Poppyseed."

"The girls will eat poppyseed?"

"I want poppyseed."

"What will the girls eat?"

"Poppyseed?" said the woman behind the counter. "Or blueberry? Just a minute."

Now she was looking at K, Jr. He smiled. She smiled. The young girls spun around. Snappy-dog raised his head. He growled. K, Jr. moved past the couple to examine banana-nut muffins. The old man said, "Girls, what kind of muffin do you want?"

"Poppyseed," said his wife.

"That's for you," said the old man. "We have to find out what the girls want. Girls, what do you want?"

"Poppyseed?" said the woman behind the counter.

"Will the you girls eat poppyseed? Will the girls eat poppyseed?" He looked at K, Jr. "Will the girls eat poppyseed?"

"I want poppyseed," the old woman said.

"Two blueberry and one poppyseed," said the old man.

The woman behind the counter bent to the display case to get the muffins. One of the little girls said, "Banana. I want banana."

"Apple," said the other.

The woman behind the counter straightened up. "Blueberry?" she said.

K, Jr. followed the exchange: the woman behind the counter, the little girls, back to the old man, to the old man's wife, the wall clock, back to the woman serving.

"Just a minute," said the woman behind the counter.

Finally the selections were made, the muffins placed on paperboard trays.

"Did you get the juices?" the old man said. He sprang toward the far end of the counter jostling K, Jr. "The juices. The girls want juices."

The order was rung up and paid for. The quartet carried their things outside to sit with the woman with the dog. K, Jr. began ordering. In a moment, the old woman was back.

"It's too cold out there. We'd like to sit inside. Is it all right if we bring the dog inside?"

"Well…" said the woman behind the counter. She appeared to be appealing to K, Jr. for help. Snappy-dog was lunging. The group had picked up all their things and were walking inside.

K, Jr. said, "Cancel my order."

"But sir, we've already started to squeeze the juice."

"Can we bring the dog inside? It'll stay on the leash."

The woman behind the counter called out. The old woman asked about the dog. The little girls laughed. Snappy-dog lunged and caught the edge of K, Jr.'s pants. Another ruin. He walked two blocks before stopping.

His girlfriend was coming out of an eyeglass store, leading Samuel. "Why aren't you at work?" she said. "Is there a problem at work? Oh, I can't take this. Now, you too."

She said that she had abandoned her bed to sleep on the ground beneath the door frame. She feared stairs, the rumbling of loud trucks. When any slight heat could change the look of things the sound of paper falling brought her to tears. Did he understand? Why save for the future when the present was less solid than smoke? Chimneys collapsed. Rooms existed in blatant disorder. Houses on stilts went sledding down hills. There was the story of the man who heard the first groaning and managed to get out the door, his home vanishing before him to tumble over a cliff.

"Can you imagine?" she said.

They spoke of insurance, security, preparation. These were concepts in the face of rocks. They inked in the kind of future planned for when describing "better days" but the definition of "normal" had altered and no one answered. What can anyone know when police lines marked the boundaries in yellow? K, Jr. said he had grown accustomed to the novelty but expected to move.

"Not you," she said. "I thought you were more solid."

It was true that bricks fell with less frequency. From that he extracted a measure of reassurance though the walls still traveled. But this was another way of shifting. There were fewer roads open, limiting access. For many, the nights remained without heat but the darkness had the power to render them mute, the lack of community exposed in the fragility of its invention. The news had grown stale. The world moved onto other bombings now as new suffering replaced the old. A surfeit of human mystery accounted for this, jolts of greater interest, better pictures. More red.

"Perhaps your hysteria is an over-reaction," he said.

"Who are you to judge?"

"We had counseling sessions at work they suggested seeking professional help to deal with this."

"Again you attack my self-esteem. Again. Oh, what do I see in you?"

"What do you see in anyone? What does anyone see in anyone?" asked Samuel.

"You're right," said K, Jr. "He has the insight of saints. Stay with him."

Their future thus imperiled, she cried. Samuel looked up at once. His lips twitched into something that might have been a smile.

"Water," he said.

Then their conversation turned to damage control, bids for restoration, discussions of different grades of paint.

She said, "I've developed a sudden interest in construction. I know how to locate the studs."

"The cats have come out of the bush to sun themselves once more."

"That's a good sign," said Ramona

"The lottery is fixed," K, Jr. said.

"We have cable."

"The bakery was untouched."

"Water," said Samuel.

"Soon," she said. Soon.

K, Jr. was able to hold onto numbers. He managed to dress. They stood a few feet apart but an opening in the sidewalk gaped between them.

"Have you ever thought about heaven?" Ramona asked. "About God? About why things happen? People change, don't they. Disaster brings out new sides of all of us."

She left him, standing, there on the sidewalk. His bones snapped with the weight of walking. The sun moved faster overhead, the neighbors argued their intentions. Ashes from a fire somewhere spread bitter across his tongue. He inhaled the dust of broken bricks, waited on crushed glass for something more to happen. Cars drove along the street. Women in workout clothing jogged up the sidewalks. Shoppers loaded down with bags came out of the shops. They laughed, walked in front of storefronts boarded up with plywood. All around them sales offered more than 50% off. Stores were going out of business. The blue curtain had moved and K, Jr. was cut off from the things he knew. He invoked the metaphor for blaming. The white dog lunged at his leg. Events lost their distinction. He had the number but had trouble remembering himself. What the day prepared night gave him, throwing him past the range of motion; he learned the corners of his room. K, Jr. turned for home. What was remembered in the space of stepping? The threshold broke, then and now merging into nothing known, perceived at the edges the outline of his life.

Then Christian called. "All is forgiven," he said. "We're supposed to go back to work. Tomorrow. I'm sure of it."

"Good," said K, Jr. "Where do we go?"

"They will tell you when you get there. Can't wait to see you. Meet me on the street and I'll take you up."

IV.

THE BLUE CURTAIN HAD MOVED and there was no getting into The Complex. All four entrances covered by blue, the bottom weighted, the curtain billowing in the breeze.

No signs signaled what to do, where to park, where to go. No information, no lights, reconstruction halted. K, Jr. found space on a side street several blocks away. The gates at each corner of The Complex were locked and he saw no way in. No Christian.

Eventually he found a service entrance, a break in the wrought-iron fences that ran the entire perimeter of The Complex. The entrance was open with no one about.

The pathways between the buildings were deserted. The trees bent in and sagged with whole limbs torn out, palm trunks marked with X's. The restoration on the buildings had ceased, empty scaffolding butting up against the outside walls. Empty dollies lay discarded by the doors, plywood sawhorses turned on their sides. There were still many broken windows boarded up. Yellow caution tapes ran around the base of a number of the buildings though the broken glass had been collected and swept up, the concrete slabs carted away, the renewal begun.

K, Jr. tried each of the doors to each of the buildings and found them locked. He placed his security card in the slot, as he had the day before but this time nothing happened. No response from the call buttons. No lights on inside any of the buildings, the shades pulled down on the ground floor offices. The doors leading downstairs to the parking garages were all locked. K, Jr. leaned in close but couldn't hear the faint booming that usually accompanied the mysterious work going on behind the blue curtain.

Under heavy cloud cover, on a gray morning of an usually dry season that wasn't dry, he worked his way from building to building, back and forth along the deserted pathways, by concrete ledges, past gentle rises of manufactured green. He stopped and called in on every one of the payphones set in black kiosks around the grounds. Christian hadn't answered his phone. No one answered the main number. K, Jr. tried every extension he remembered, tried the voice mail number.

He sat for a long time on the brick ledge of one of the planters near the fountain. This morning no water poured, the pool empty. The dirty tiles had cracks along the bottom. It looked like earth showing through.

The sun appeared briefly at noon, moved across the sky, visible between the buildings, then out of sight as the afternoon wore on. The temperature began to drop. K, Jr. buttoned his coat.

He was thinking of finding the service entrance again, about getting out of The Complex, having to look for another job, leaving the city. Voices.

The three men from Maintenance came down the path. They carried nothing with them. They walked in single file wearing white jump suits, the patch over their hearts bearing their names. They came up the three steps of the deck and sat in a circle around him, crossing their legs. They introduced themselves, in English, as Effraim—the man usually with the ladder, Martín—the man with the box, and Joachim—the man with the bulbs.

"Do you know where everyone is?" K, Jr. said. "Why I can't get in the buildings. No one answers. No phones. Are we through? Do we have a future? Where are we going from here?"

"We're going to tell you, K," said Martín. "Everything you need to know."

"You have but one father," Joachim said.

"Huh. Central Distribution at The Complex. You spoke English all along. Damn you. This is a joke."

"I will talk to you because you have conquered the evil one," Joachim said. "But take not the Lord's name in vain or anyone's."

"Be aware, keep alert," said Martín. "You do not know when the time will come."

"My little K," Joachim said. "I am telling these things to you so that you may not sin. But if anyone does sin, we have an advocate within the Central Distribution. You are surprised that it is Rex Christian. He has been chosen."

"Christian? What are you all talking about? This city is in trouble. We're trying to repair. I know. I went out with blankets and food. People are hurting."

"Go up, K, Jr.," said Effraim. "Kill and eat."

They stood together and walked away, each after bowing to him. By now it was approaching sunset. K, Jr. found the service entrance and left The Complex.

The blue curtain still covered the entrances. No booming, no wind, no mysterious billowing, the streets empty. K, Jr. walked down to the entrance and to the curtain. No one stopped him, no one turned him back.

Voices called to him. Ramona and Christian stood on opposites sides of the street. She was in black and Christian was in white—robes maybe, or designer sweat suits.

"K, Jr.," they called. "We're going."

"Come with me," Ramona said.

Christian put his hand on his chest. "I'm here to take you up."

K, Jr. waited for the light to change, then for a sign. The city was as clear as he had ever seen it. To the west the ocean sparkled with the motion of a billion lights, the sun starting to catch at the horizon, the pinks and flaming oranges coming on. To the east Mt. Wilson stood out, a tower capped by snow.

Then he ripped aside the curtain and entered the first level of the parking structure.

Empty and forlorn and sporadically lit, a new breeze rippled through, making the curtain billow. There was only the sound of the wind, no more human voices, and the blue curtain covering the door.

About the Author

IAN RANDALL WILSON's short stories and poetry have appeared in many journals including *The New Mexico Humanities Review*, *The Alaska Quarterly Review*, *The Mid-American Review*, and the *North American Review*. He is on the faculty at the UCLA Extension and lives in Los Angeles.

www.ingramcontent.com/pod-product-compliance
Lightning Source LLC
Chambersburg PA
CBHW051926240626
47153CB00004B/1389